W9-AVR-147

# Olly Spellmaker
## Elf Alert!

Susan Price started writing and telling stories when she was very young – and was winning prizes for it from the age of fourteen. Her first novel, *The Devil's Piper*, was bought by a publisher when she was sixteen. Since then, she has had lots of jobs and written many books for children and young adults, including *The Sterkarm Handshake* (which won the Guardian Children's Fiction Award) and *The Ghost Drum* (which won the Carnegie Medal).

*Also by Susan Price from Macmillan*

Olly Spellmaker and the Hairy Horror
Olly Spellmaker and the Sulky Smudge

# Olly Spellmaker
## Elf Alert!

*Susan Price*

*Illustrated by David Roberts*

MACMILLAN CHILDREN'S BOOKS

First published 2005 by Macmillan Children's Books
a division of Macmillan Publishers Ltd
20 New Wharf Road, London N1 9RR
Basingstoke and Oxford
www.panmacmillan.com

Associated companies throughout the world

ISBN 0 330 42123 9

Text copyright © Susan Price 2005
Illustrations copyright © David Roberts 2005

The right of Susan Price and David Roberts to be identified as the
author and illustrator of this work has been asserted by them in accordance
with the Copyright, Designs and Patents Act 1988.

All rights reserved. No part of this publication may be
reproduced, stored in or introduced into a retrieval system, or
transmitted, in any form, or by any means (electronic, mechanical,
photocopying, recording or otherwise) without the prior written
permission of the publisher. Any person who does any unauthorized
act in relation to this publication may be liable to criminal
prosecution and civil claims for damages.

1 3 5 7 9 8 6 4 2

A CIP catalogue record for this book is
available from the British Library.

Printed and bound in Great Britain by Mackays of Chatham plc, Kent

This book is sold subject to the condition that it shall not,
by way of trade or otherwise, be lent, resold, hired out,
or otherwise circulated without the publisher's prior consent
in any form of binding or cover other than that in which
it is published and without a similar condition including this
condition being imposed on the subsequent purchaser.

# Contents

# 1. Muddy Footprints

Alex Langford's dad said to him, 'Haven't we asked you not to stuff crisp packets down the sides of the chairs? Didn't we say we'd try to keep the house a bit tidy while your mother's away?'

'I didn't put crisp packets down the chairs!' Alex said.

'What are these, then?' His dad held up three crumpled, empty packets.

'"Salt and vinegar",' Alex said. '"Cheese and onion", "Smoky bacon" – you *know* I only like plain crisps. It's you and Mum who eat all the others.'

'Ah, well,' said his dad, looking guilty. 'I don't stick 'em down the sides of the chairs!'

1

'No – you roll 'em up, chuck 'em at the waste-paper bin, and miss! And then Mum has to pick 'em up and gets mad.'

'Well, your mother's not here,' his dad said, 'so try and keep things tidy!'

Alex stared after him. 'I didn't do it! I am being tidy!'

'Don't do it again!' his dad said, which made Alex furious.

His dad was so irritable that Alex could only think he was missing Kirsty, Alex's mum, who'd been gone for three days now. She'd driven all the way to Scotland, to visit her family. Alex thought he might miss her himself in a few more days' time, but just now, things were peaceful – or would have been, if his dad hadn't started accusing him of doing things he hadn't done.

That evening, only a few hours later, his dad said, 'Have you had that piece of pork pie I left in the fridge?'

'Now why would I have done that?' Alex asked.

'Have you had it?'

'I hate pork pie!'

'Well, where's it gone then?'

'You must have eaten it.'

'I didn't,' his dad said. 'I was looking forward to that pork pie. I'm put out.'

'Well, I haven't had it,' Alex said. 'Stop going on at me about things I haven't done.'

'Hmm,' his dad said, in a way which meant he thought Alex *had* eaten the pork pie. Which made Alex furious again.

But he forgave his dad when they went to the supermarket to do a big shop, because Rob let him buy lots of fizzy drinks, and different kinds of crisps, and sweets, and things that Kirsty never let him have. She said they were 'refined rubbish', full of E-numbers, whatever they were, and 'empty calories'. But Rob said, 'Once in a while won't hurt us,' and put a packet of sugary cereal in the trolley instead of porridge. 'It's about time us English broke free of Scottish oppression. Freedom!'

3

Next morning, Alex was washing the cups and bowls from breakfast. He'd agreed with his dad that, while his mum was away, they'd keep everything clean and in order, so there'd be nothing for her to complain about when she got back. So Alex was washing up, while looking out of the window at the garden. He wasn't looking *at* anything – just staring. But something rose up out of the general muddle of leaves and grass. It was bright red, and that made him notice it. He realized that he was looking at a garden gnome wearing a red hat.

He put down the cup he was washing, and took a better look.

A small, bearded gnome was standing by the lavender bush at the edge of the path. As well as the red hat, it wore trousers, a shirt and waistcoat, and carried a basket on its back.

Alex went into the other room, where his dad was vacuuming. 'When did you buy the garden gnome?'

Rob turned the cleaner off. 'What?'

'The garden gnome – when did you buy it?'

'What garden gnome?'

'The one in the garden!'

Rob went to the window. 'There's no gnome in the garden.'

And, when Alex looked, there wasn't. 'But it was there, by the path.'

'Isn't there now,' Rob said.

'Maybe Mum bought it.'

'*Kirsty?* Buy a *garden gnome*?'

'As a joke?' Alex said.

'You're the one who's joking, pal. You're seeing things.'

Alex went back to the washing-up in disgust.

The day after that, Alex got up and was on his way to the kitchen for breakfast, when he heard chatter coming from the living room. It was the television.

Funny, he thought, standing in the hall. It was a Sunday. He'd thought his dad was still in bed.

He went into the living room. The curtains were still closed, but the television was on. His dad wasn't in there.

Alex switched the television off and drew the curtains. When he turned, he saw an empty crisp packet, a chocolate wrapper and a banana skin lying on the table.

Oh, Dad, he thought, shaking his head. This isn't keeping your end of our agreement. And leaving the television on all night, wasting electricity – Mum would have a *lot* to say about that if she was at home. He quite looked forward to having a go at his dad about it himself.

Alex gathered up the rubbish, feeling very smug, and went through into the kitchen. He'd put the rubbish in the bin and opened the blind before he noticed the muddy footprints on the floor. They tracked between the

door into the yard, and the kitchen door into the hall. The prints of muddy boots. Very small muddy boots. Smaller than his own.

He tried the kitchen door. It was locked. But then, looking down, Alex noticed something he'd forgotten – their door had a cat flap. They didn't have a cat, but the people his mum and dad had bought the house from had had one, and Rob and Kirsty had never bothered to change the door. Occasionally one or another of the neighbourhood cats came through, visiting or scrounging. But none of these cats, as far as Alex knew, wore little boots.

Standing in the kitchen, he thought, Crisp packets down the chairs? Pork pie missing? Television left on and little muddy footprints on the floor? Gnomes appearing and disappearing? This is getting peculiar.

This, he thought, is something I should ask Olly Spellmaker about.

Olly Spellmaker was a witch, but she rode a motorbike instead of a broomstick. She'd been a great help to them when their house was being redecorated against their will by a bogle. But then she'd dragged Alex into a scheme to supply an unhaunted pub with some ghosts, and *that* had gone a bit pear-shaped. And Olly would keep telling Alex that he was a witch too, when Alex didn't *want* to be a witch.

No. Best say nothing to Olly. There was bound to be some sensible explanation for the little muddy footprints and all the other things going on. Maybe the neighbourhood cats *had* started wearing little boots and stealing pork pie out of fridges, and he just hadn't noticed before.

He made a cup of tea and took it up to his dad. When Rob heard his bedroom door being pushed open, he reared up from under his duvet with a groan and his hair all on end.

'What? Tea? Grand. What's this for?'

'You left the telly on all night,' Alex said, testing.

'Did I?' Rob took a gulp of tea. 'Ahh!'

'And you left banana skins and chocolate wrappers and crisp packets everywhere.'

'Left them where?'

'Downstairs. On the table. I thought we were going to keep the place tidy.'

Rob was still frowning. 'I haven't had a banana. Or crisps or chocolate, come to that.'

'You didn't eat stuff last night before you came to bed?'

Rob sat up straighter. 'No. After that

shepherd's pie, I didn't want anything. And I switched the television off! It was only about eleven when I came up, and I remember switching it off.'

Alex sat down on the edge of the bed. 'Dad, I think there's something weird going on. Remember how I saw that gnome in the garden? Well, there's all these funny little footprints on the kitchen floor . . .'

Rob stared. 'Oh, no.'

'Do you think we should call Olly?'

'Oh, no, not yet.' Neither Kirsty nor Rob approved of Olly Spellmaker much. They thought she was a bit cracked.

'But, Dad – gnomes appearing, footprints, your pork pie vanishing . . .'

'Yeah, well . . . Nothing else might happen. But if you bring Olly into it, things will happen with bells and knobs on. They always do, when she's around.'

So they didn't call Olly. And something else happened the very next night.

10

# 2. Somebody Downstairs

Alex woke in the night. He'd had a hard time getting to sleep in the first place, and then he'd been dreaming of wandering pork pies and dancing crisp packets. He felt as tired as if he'd never been asleep at all.

Wearily, he got out of bed and trudged to the bathroom. On his way back, he was shocked to a halt by a scream. From downstairs. A second later he realized it was the television. His dad must be watching a horror film.

He looked at his watch. Ten past three. Was his dad still up?

He went to Rob's bedroom door and gently pushed it open. Inside it was dark and had that Dad smell – 'Like the rangy-tangy pen at the zoo,' his gran always said. He could hear his dad breathing, with just a hint of a snore.

Alex went back to the landing, leaned on the banister and listened. Pounding, dramatic music boomed from the living room. His dad was getting really careless about switching the telly off.

And then came a roar of laughter from downstairs. Not television laughter. *Real* laughter.

The palms of his hands itched, and then his thumbs itched and tingled. The feeling spread through his hands, ran up his arms, up the back of his neck, and made his scalp itch and tingle too. It was the strongest twingle he'd ever had, and he thought, Oh, no! I'm turning into a witch!

Alex realized that, from the moment he'd woken, he'd been twingling, but he hadn't been paying attention. Now he couldn't ignore it. The twingle meant that there was something supernatural or magical near –

ghosts, or goblins, or something that laughed at television in the night.

Alex pulled back from the banister, scared. He went back into his dad's bedroom and jumped on the bed. 'Dad! Dad!'

'Unh? What?'

'Dad, there's something downstairs!'

'Alex! It's the middle of the night! What . . . ?'

'There's something downstairs!'

They both lay still and listened. Faintly, the music from the television filtered to them. Alex could tell by his dad's face that he could hear it too.

'I'll call the police,' Rob said, and rolled across the bed to reach for his mobile.

'No!' Alex said.

'Why not?'

Alex's hands and arms, his scalp and even his ears, were still twingling. He knew that whatever was downstairs wasn't something the police could deal with. 'I'll go and see what it is,' he said, and left the room.

13

'Alex! No!' Rob got out of bed.

Together they crept down the stairs. The sound of the television grew louder. So did the laughter. Alex looked back and was alarmed to see how angry his dad was. He hardly looked like Rob at all.

They sidled along the hall, and Rob pulled Alex back, and stepped in front of him, so that he would reach the door of the living room first. Alex didn't know whether to be glad that his dad was protecting him or annoyed that he wasn't going to be the first to

see what was on the other side of the living-room door.

From behind the door came a burst of car engines and gunfire and then mocking laughter.

Rob gently pushed the door open with his finger, poked his head forward, and peered through the crack.

He pulled his head back and looked at Alex, astonished. Then he guided Alex forward so that he could peer into the room.

# 3. Garden Gnomes

The television was showing some sort of noisy car-chase film, with cars flying over hump-back bridges, engines screaming.

On the floor near the low coffee table was an open can of orangeade with four long straws in it, and on the edge of the table was an open packet of crisps. Parked near the sofa was a little green wheelbarrow holding another can of drink and a packet of nuts and raisins.

And there, sitting on the sofa in a row, were four garden gnomes, watching the film and guffawing. As Alex watched, one of them leaned forward, took a straw in his mouth and sucked up a good slug of fizzy drink. Before

he leaned back, he belched loudly and helped himself to a couple of crisps.

Alex backed into the hall, letting the living-room door close gently. He looked bemusedly at his dad. Rob was mad, it was easy to see that.

Rob opened his mouth and closed it again two or three times, as if he wanted to say something but couldn't think what. Then he smacked the door open with the flat of his hand making a loud noise that made Alex jump, and shouldered into the room in a rugby charge, yelling, 'Right, you little toerags – let's be having yer!'

Alex, diving in behind his father, saw the gnomes leaping off the sofa, beards flying, all going different ways. Rob tried to grab one, missed, tried to grab another, but they scattered, some diving under the coffee table, some running round the sofa. 'Come here!' Rob was yelling.

Alex saw a gnome scurrying for the door, so he slammed it shut. Rob heard the noise, and shouted, 'Gotcha! Owwwww!'

One of the gnomes had run in and kicked him hard on the shin. While Rob stood on one leg to rub his sore shin, another gnome seized the handles of the wheelbarrow and ran it hard into the leg he was standing on. Rob howled and fell backwards into an armchair.

'Hey!' Alex said, as he made a grab for the

gnome with the wheelbarrow – and felt a pain in his own leg. He looked down and saw that another gnome had hold of his leg and was biting him! *Biting* him!

He shook his leg, but the little man held on, and it hurt – and here came another one, running at him – what was that one going to do?

Alex panicked and opened the living-room door. The gnomes raised a shout – the one on Alex's leg let go – and they all ran into the hall and kitchen.

'Don't let them get away!' Rob heaved himself up from the chair and ran after them. Alex followed.

In the kitchen, a little bum was sticking out of the cat flap, little legs kicking as they struggled to push the bum through. 'Aha!' Rob said and pounced down and

grabbed the legs. With some effort, as the legs kicked, he dragged the gnome back through the cat flap.

Rob straightened, holding the gnome up by the scruff of his neck. Swinging round, he shoved the creature at Alex. 'Here, catch hold of this!'

Startled, Alex clutched at the chunky, hot, solid little body. His face was filled with harsh hair and a smell of earth and wood smoke. The body kicked, punched and wriggled so that Alex nearly dropped it. He had to hug it tight to keep hold. It weighed about as much as a big, heavy cat.

'I'll get the others!' Rob said, struggling with the lock of the back door. He yanked it open, but before he could go through it, several gnomes ran through the widening gap. The one in the lead lugged a trowel, the one behind him had a length of cane.

'Ow!' The one with a trowel whacked Rob on the shin, a good hard whack. The one with the cane whipped him round the legs. Just the sound of it made Alex wince. Still clutching the wriggling gnome he'd been given, he backed into the living room.

'I'll . . .' Rob, hopping and flinching, was trying to dodge the gnomes or kick them, but their attack was fierce. With a yell, he jumped back through the living-room door and slammed it shut.

The gnome in Alex's arms twisted and squirmed right out of Alex's hold, dropped to the floor and ran away. Alex didn't see where he went – he was too busy watching his dad, who was leaning on the door as it creaked and shook under the blows from the other side. Alex put his fingers in his ears.

Then everything went quiet. Alex supposed that the gnomes on the other side of the door were tired and out of breath.

In the silence, a strange voice said, 'Oh dearie, dearie me.'

Rob and Alex turned. The gnome they'd

captured was standing on the coffee table with his arms folded. 'Well now, my big, bold mannie,' he said to Rob. 'You've got yourself in a right good deep hole, haven't yer now?'

# 4. Runstrewel, Kernoggle, Gobalt and Dalgren

Rob set his back against the living-room door. 'Are you talking to me?'

Alex was staring at the gnome. He was about two feet high and solidly built. If he'd been the same height as Rob, he'd have been much the heavier. He had a black beard, streaked with grey, and longish dark hair, but the very top of his head was bald. He was dressed in trousers of a thick, hard-wearing material, with a broad, buckled leather belt, and a blue shirt with sweat marks under the arms. There were no boots on his feet, just worn, faded blue socks.

'Be sure I'm talking to you, my mannie! What are you going to do now, eh? Trapped in your own trap!'

23

Rob wagged his finger at the little man. 'Listen, titch. You're not so well off yourself. You're all on your own on this side of the door.'

'Do you see me wetting meself?' the little man asked.

They all just looked at each other.

What a situation, Alex thought. There they were, in the middle of the night, in their own living room. Alex was wearing just a saggy, baggy pair of pyjama bottoms; and Rob nothing except boxer shorts and socks. Trapped, in their own home, by a gang of thuggish garden gnomes.

'Look,' Alex said, 'what are we going to do about this?'

His dad and the gnome looked at him.

'We're stuck in here,' he said to his dad. 'And you –' he looked at the gnome – 'you're stuck in here. So . . . how are we going to sort this out? What do you want? This is *our* house, you know.'

'*Your* house?' said the gnome. 'Oh, aye? And whose land is it?'

'Mine!' Rob said. 'Well, mine and . . . my partner's. We bought it.'

'Bought it!' said the gnome. 'Who sold it to you? We didn't – and it's ours!'

The hammering started on the door again, with the added sounds of kicking and punching. Rob tried to say something, but he couldn't be heard. The gnome hopped down from the table, ran across the floor past Rob's knees and gave the door a hefty kick. 'Whisht yer noise!' he yelled. 'We're trying to have an argument in here!' The noise from outside stopped, and the gnome turned from the door, folded his arms and looked up . . . and up and up at Rob. 'So what badger sold you our land?'

'It's not *your* land!' Rob said. 'You're a . . . garden gnome! The most you own is a fishing rod!'

'Oh, is that right?' said the gnome. 'What's the name of this place?'

'It hasn't got a name,' Rob said. 'It's just our house.'

The gnome rolled his eyes and looked at Alex. 'You seem a smart lad. What's this place called?'

Alex frowned. He opened his mouth to answer, and then wondered what he was doing, standing in his pyjama bottoms in the middle of the night answering a garden gnome's questions. Was he dreaming?

The gnome frowned.

'Thorn Hill Road?' Alex asked.

'Thorn Hill Road! Right you are! And why is it called Thorn Hill Road?'

'Er . . . because it's on a hill?'

'Good, aye, it's a hill. And the thorn part?'

'There were thorns on it once? Thorn bushes?'

'Very good!' said the gnome, and looked at Rob. 'He your son?' Rob nodded. 'What does he get from you? Cos it's neither looks nor brains.'

'You're not making any friends,' Rob said. 'What's all the gabble about thorns and hills?'

'This was one of our ancestral hills!' said the gnome, stamping his foot for emphasis. 'We always grew thorns on our hills. So we've come back here. Where do you expect us to go?'

'Away!' Rob yelled.

'Where have you come back from?' Alex asked.

'Oh, a long way off,' said the gnome. 'This hill got too crowded, see – and there was kirk bells clanging and too many of you big yins around. So we left. But now we've come back.'

Alex's mum was Scottish, so he knew that a 'kirk' was a church and that 'big yin' meant 'big one'. 'When did you leave?' he asked.

'Oh . . . three hundred . . . no, more like four hundred year ago. Call it five hundred.'

Alex and Rob stared at each other.

'There's even more of us "big yins" around

now,' Rob said. 'You'd best leave again.'

'Oh, there's big yins everywhere now,' said the gnome. 'We'll just have to lump it.'

From the other side of the door a voice shouted, 'Runstrewel?' There was a rapping on the door. 'Are you all right in there?'

'Don't worry about me,' the gnome shouted back. 'I'm just having a bit chat with they big yins.'

'Is that your name – Runstrewel?' Alex said. 'Mine's Alex. This is my dad, Rob.'

'Aye,' said the gnome, 'but let's not get too friendly just yet. We've some things to sort out.'

'Tell you what,' Alex said, 'if we let the others in, will they promise not to attack us?'

'Will you promise not to attack *us*?'

'We weren't attacking anybody,' Rob said. 'We were trying to apprehend intruders.'

'We promise,' Alex said. 'Truce. Nobody has a go at anybody.'

'All right, then, promise,' said the gnome.

He went over to the door and had a word through it with those on the other side; and when they'd agreed, in trooped three more gnomes.

'What's going on, then?' one of them asked.

'It was a misunderstanding,' Alex said. 'We're sorry we attacked you.' He glanced at his father. From the way Rob was standing, with his arms folded, Alex guessed that he didn't feel a bit sorry and didn't think there'd been a misunderstanding either.

'They didn't know this used to be our hill,' said Runstrewel. 'Alex, Rob, this is Kernoggle.'

Kernoggle held up his hand and shook Alex's finger. He was an old-looking gnome, with a thick head of white hair and a thick white beard – a bit like a miniature Santa Claus. Alex was fascinated by his little spectacles. Did gnomes have gnome opticians?

'How do,' Rob said with a nod, not unfolding his arms.

'I'm Dalgren, lad, pleased to meet you,' said a red-faced gnome with dark, curly hair and a big grin. 'How are you, big yin – is it sunny up there?'

Rob barely nodded.

'And I'm Gobalt,' said the last gnome, shaking Alex's finger. He had a neatly trimmed grey beard and was bald except for a little fringe of hair round his ears.

'Ah, well, let's get back to business,' said Dalgren, hopping back up on to the sofa and reaching for the control.

'Going to join us?' Runstrewel asked Alex. 'Got any peanuts?'

Rob unfolded his arms. 'Now just a minute . . .'

The gnomes all turned and looked at him.

'You can't just carry on,' Rob said.

'Why not?' Runstrewel asked.

'Because we're trying to sleep! And this is our house! And that's my electricity. And my food!'

The gnomes seemed astonished. Runstrewel nudged Alex in the leg and said, 'A bit stingy, your dad, had you noticed?'

'And what's more,' Rob said, 'my partner, Kirsty, will be back at the end of the week. And she won't want to find you lot here.'

'Oh, no!' Alex said. He hadn't really thought about his mum coming back until then, but Rob was right. When Kirsty found her house full of uninvited garden gnomes, she would be . . . well, not a bit pleased. Kirsty didn't like ghosts or bogles or house-spirits, and Alex was pretty sure she wouldn't like gnomes either.

'Is Kirsty a lady?' Dalgren asked with a big grin. 'I'll talk her round, don't worry.'

Alex felt even more worried. 'When Mum's put out,' he said, 'well . . .' When Kirsty was annoyed, she made it very, very clear to everyone around her that she was annoyed, and why, and what she wanted done about it. Trying to talk her round was never a good idea.

'You've got to go before Mum comes back,' Alex said.

The gnomes had all settled back on the sofa. 'We've nowhere else to go, child,' said Kernoggle, 'even if we wanted to go anywhere else, which we don't. Some biscuits would be nice, you reckon? I fancy something sweet.'

'Alex,' Rob said, 'come upstairs.' Alex followed his dad out of the room. The gnomes took no notice.

Upstairs, Rob took his mobile phone from his belt and passed it to Alex. 'Phone Olly.'

'What? In the middle of the night?'

'She's a witch, isn't she? She's probably up and about, flying round on her broomstick. Anyway, this is an emergency.'

Alex held the phone. 'I dunno . . .'

'Think about your mother coming back and finding *them*. She'll have our innards out and chop 'em up for haggis.'

Alex dialled Olly's number. It rang and rang. 'She's not answering. Either she's asleep

or . . .' He turned the phone off. 'I just remembered.'

'What?'

'Olly's gone away for a couple of days. To a
witches' convention.'

'You're kidding,' Rob said.

'No. Lots of witches meet up at a hotel and
tell each other about how they do spells.' His
dad was staring at him. 'Really.'

'Well, when's she coming back?'

'Not sure.'

'What are we going to do?'

'I can send her an email,' Alex said. 'She'll
be checking them from the hotel. I'll ask her to
come over as soon as she gets back.'

'Please,' Rob said, 'please let it be before
your mother comes home.'

# 5. Gnomes Behaving Badly

---

**From:**        Alex34@spruce.co.uk
**Subject:**     Help!

Olly – our place is full of garden gnomes. They're eating us out of house and home, and Mum will be back soon! We need your help!

---

**From:**        o.spellmaker@geist.co.uk
**Subject:**     Gnomes?!?!?

Oh la la la! What larks!

Well, Alex thought, as he read this, that's not a lot of use. Trust Olly to just say something silly.

Meanwhile, their home was still full of garden gnomes, and they didn't just sneak into the house at night now – they came in any time they liked. 'You know about us,' Runstrewel said, 'so why bother to hide?'

When Alex got up, he would find them lying about on the sofa, snoring. When he drew the curtains, they'd wake up, cover their eyes and groan and call him names. If he wanted the television or radio on, they grumbled and made a fuss, because of their headaches.

'If you didn't drink litres and litres of *our* drinks,' Alex said, 'and if you didn't eat crisps and sweets and rubbish all the time – *our* rubbish! Oh! I mean . . . !'

Despite feeling ill, the gnomes pointed at him, laughing and jeering.

'Well, me and Dad do eat some other things as well! We don't just eat sugar and junk food! That's why *we* don't have headaches and bellyaches all the time!' Listen to me, he thought, and felt embarrassed. He sounded like his mother.

The gnomes helped themselves to food whenever they felt like it, by clambering up the kitchen units like mountaineers or using one of Alex's rulers to lever open the fridge. They were very strong and agile, although they looked so small and old.

Alex went into the kitchen one morning to find Gobalt and Runstrewel standing on top of the worktop. They had a loaf of bread open, with slices tumbling out of the packet. Gobalt had taken the lid off a tub of margarine and was spooning the greasy stuff on to a slice of bread, while Runstrewel wielded a knife and did the spreading.

Hearing Alex, they both looked round. 'Get butter, will you?' Runstrewel said. 'This stuff is no good, no good at all.'

'Give me the money for it and maybe we will,' Alex said.

'Money, money,' Gobalt said, shaking his head. 'All you big yins think about is your money.'

They finished spreading the margarine and put the greasy spoon and knife down on the worktop.

'You're making a mess!' Alex said, thinking of his mother. Kirsty made plenty of mess herself, but was furious when anybody else did.

'Nag, nag, nag,' Runstrewel said, wrapping his arms round a jar of jam, to steady it. Gobalt got hold of the jar's lid and twisted it off. Then he held the jar and tilted it to one side, while Runstrewel got the spoon and spooned jam from the jar on to the bread. Jam dribbled from the spoon and the bread. And all the time the gnomes were trampling about in their muddy boots.

Alex thought how he would like to grab them by the scruffs of their necks and throw them out of the door. For a moment or two his hands twitched with the intention of doing it – but in the end he was too scared. They were small, but they were tough little nuts. He knew that they could bite.

If the gnomes were annoying during the day, they were worse in the evening. They would all come in, climb on the sofa and sit in a row, so Rob had to move to an armchair and Alex had to sit on the other side of the room, in the other armchair. The only other choice was to sit on the floor, which was draughty and uncomfortable. It felt as if they were visitors in their own house. They could order the gnomes off the sofa, of course, but they both knew that the gnomes wouldn't move. What then? To try and move the gnomes by force could turn into a nasty tussle.

'Some cans of drink and crisps would be nice,' Dalgren said that evening.

'It would,' Rob agreed. 'Why don't you go down the road and buy yourself some?'

'Nah,' Runstrewel said, 'let's me and you go and get some out the kitchen, Dal.' Dalgren and Runstrewel hopped off the sofa and headed for the kitchen.

Alex looked across at his dad and saw Rob

glowering straight ahead, furious, but unable to think of anything to do.

The gnomes fetched the drinks and crisps in their wheelbarrow. They were slurping drinks and belching loudly and crunching crisps when Rob said, 'The news is on. Where's the control?' He was looking under the cushions of his chair. 'Can't see it.'

Alex looked around, checking under his own cushions and among the cups on the table. Then he noticed the gnomes, and the way they were glancing at each other, with little smiles. 'They've got it,' he said.

'Got what?' Runstrewel demanded.

'You know what,' Rob said. 'The TV control.'

'What's one of them?' Kernoggle asked.

'Oh, you know!' Alex said. 'Stop playing about.'

'Don't know what you're talking about,' Runstrewel said. 'Do you, Dal?'

'No! How about you, Gob?'

'Never seen it,' Gobalt said.

'Put the news on,' Rob said.

'You don't want to see the news,' Runstrewel said. 'There's dolphins on here in a minute.'

'And wildebeest after,' said Gobalt.

'I'm sick to death of dolphins!' Rob said. 'Every time I blink you gnomes are watching another pesterin' programme about faffing dolphins and how pesterin' clever they are. I'm up to here with dolphins! And if I never see another wildebeest crossing a river, it'll be too soon.'

Alex kept quiet. He felt that he ought to be on his dad's side, but he would much rather watch dolphins and wildebeest than the news.

Rob suffered the dolphins for a while, but then he got up and went over to the sofa and started searching among the cushions. He couldn't find the control.

'They're passing it from one to the other,' Alex said. He'd been watching the little shifty movements of the gnomes.

'We are not!' Runstrewel said.

Rob gave up and angrily sat down again. He knew that he wasn't going to get the control without fighting for it. While Alex and the gnomes watched the dolphins and the wildebeest, Rob picked up a newspaper and read it fiercely. But when the final wildebeest had, at last, fallen into the river, he threw his newspaper down and said, 'Right! The footy's just started.'

'Ach,' said Kernoggle, 'who in the world wants to watch twenty-two doughnuts of big yins running about after a ball?'

'The gardening's on the other side,' said Dalgren, and the others all said, 'Oh, aye!'

'It's about dahlias!'

'Stick that on!'

Alex couldn't tell which gnome had the control, but one of them did, and the channel changed to the programme about gardening: tips about mulching and spring bulbs.

'Just look at them dahlias!' said Dalgren.

'The strength of colour!'

'The size of them heads!' said Kernoggle.

'Aye,' said the other two dreamily. 'Aye.'

Rob got up and left the room. He slammed the door a bit.

'You've made Dad mad now,' Alex said. 'He pays for all those crisps and cans of fizzy drinks you guzzle, you know.'

'It's our ancestral land,' Runstrewel said, 'since before you big yins were around at all. So let your whingeing be.'

Alex went upstairs to see how his dad was. Rob was lying on his bed watching the football on the little portable TV. He seemed glum, despite his team being one up. When Alex sat down beside him, he said, 'I dread your mother coming back.'

Alex could only sigh, nod and agree.

So when, the next day, there was a knock on the door and Alex opened it to see Olly Spellmaker standing there, he said, 'Oh, am I glad you're here!'

She filled the doorway, a big block of black motorcycle leathers. 'Well, ditto!' she said. 'Couldn't be more glad to *be* here, little pal of mine!' She tugged off her helmet, leaving her short black hair sticking up in all directions, and gave him a big grin. Her lipstick was very red, her eyes were outlined with thick black lines and her earrings were silver dragons, made in sections, one behind another, so that the dragons' heads nodded, their front and back legs waggled and

44

their little pointed tails wagged.

'Come in,' Alex said. 'Come in quick and meet the blasted gnomes.'

Olly came in, creaking and squeaking in her leathers, and Alex led her into the sitting room, where Dalgren and Runstrewel were lying end to end on the sofa, gently snoring.

'So these are they?' Olly said, looking at them with interest. 'Strictly speaking, darling, it's not garden gnomes you have here, it's earth-elves. Sure you want rid of 'em? They'll do wonders for your herbaceous border – spirits of the earth and all that.'

The door was pushed open and Kernoggle came in, carrying a banana over his shoulder. 'Aha!' he said. 'Another witch!'

'Blessings be, petal',' Olly said.

Alex said, 'What do you mean, "another witch"?'

Kernoggle put down his banana and stared up at him. 'You're a witch, aren't you?'

'I am not a witch!' Alex said. 'I keep telling

people I'm not a witch and I don't want to be a witch! Why doesn't anybody listen?'

Kernoggle looked up at Olly and said, 'Hark at him.'

'We know you're not a witch, precious,' Olly said. 'You couldn't cast a spell for cash down. You're just a teensy bit witchy round the edges, that's all.'

Alex felt hurt. He wanted to say, I *am* a witch, really; or I could be, if I felt like it. Because he did have these things Olly called 'twingles'. His palms and thumbs itched and tingled when there were ghosts or anything supernatural about. When Olly asked him if he wanted to be a witch, he always said loudly that, no, he didn't; and he didn't want to twingle – but, secretly, he was quite proud of it. Secretly, he thought that it might be fun to be a witch sometimes – so long as he could still be a computer programmer when he grew up. But he couldn't admit that to Olly, so he just said, to Kernoggle, 'Where's the other one?'

The door was shoved open again, and in came Gobalt, pushing a small green wheelbarrow loaded with crisps and a can of drink.

'Is this "the other one"?' Olly asked. 'Pleased to meet you, mate – I'm Olly Spellmaker. Ooh . . . cheesy crisps! Ta very much!'

Gobalt blinked as she took a packet of crisps from his barrow, and looked at Kernoggle to see what he should do.

'Never mind,' Kernoggle said. 'If my guess is right, Madam Witch has come to turf us out, on behalf of the other big yins. Am I right, Madam Witch?'

'Turf you out? Not at all.

Not my style, darlin'. Think of me as agony aunt to elf and goblin.'

'What's an agony aunt?' Gobalt whispered to Kernoggle, who shrugged.

'One who listens to your problems and soothes and solves them,' Olly said. 'Let's all sit down together and put up our collective feet. A nice cup of tea and some biscuits – of the chocolate-coated sort, Alex, petal – would be very helpful indeed. While chomping on the chocolate bicky of peace, let's hear your tale of how you came to fetch up here, and why. And wherefore, and all that lark. And then we shall be wiser than we are now and shall see what we shall see.'

Gobalt and Kernoggle looked at each other.

'Has she stopped?' Gobalt asked.

'I think so,' Kernoggle said. 'We'd better wake up that pair of doughnuts.'

# 6. Kenelmsfell

'Well, you'll remember how it was,' Kernoggle said, 'when the big yins started building the kirks and hanging the ding-dongs in the towers . . .'

'Not personally, no,' Olly said. 'Just a tad before my time.'

'By about a year,' Alex said.

'Ignore him. He's just annoyed because we're eating all the biscuits.'

'He's the same as all you big yins, then,' said Runstrewel. 'Forever thinking of your bellies.' He helped himself to another biscuit, while pressing a hand to his head.

All four gnomes – or elves, or whatever they were – were sitting on the sofa, eating.

Dalgren and Runstrewel kept complaining that they didn't feel well.

Olly was in one armchair, and Alex in another.

'Big yins stopped believing in us,' Kernoggle said. 'Instead of coming along to us with their problems, they went to the kirk.'

'Them ding-dongs made a horrible noise,' Gobalt said. 'Went right through yer.'

'Right you are!' Runstrewel agreed. 'I couldn't stand it!'

'None of us could,' Kernoggle said. 'So we left – we went west, to another hill. That was years and years ago.'

'Something like a thousand years ago. Or more,' Olly said quietly to Alex. 'They live longer than us.'

'Lives as short as yours are hardly worth living,' Runstrewel said.

'We beg to differ, darling,' Olly said. 'So, was it good, this other hill?'

'Oh, fine, fine,' Kernoggle said. 'For a good

long time it was fine. But you know how it is.'

'You had a falling out,' Olly said.

Dalgren, who was obviously feeling better, sat up straighter, smoothed down his curly hair and beamed at Olly. 'It was over the *ladies*,' he said.

'Not enough of 'em,' said Runstrewel, his head in his hands. He obviously wasn't feeling better.

'A lot of bad feeling,' Kernoggle said, 'so we started thinking about our ancestral hill.'

'And back we came!' said Dalgren, still beaming at Olly.

'But there's nothing here,' Gobalt said. 'Just big yins' houses.'

'You forget, when you're in the hill,' Kernoggle said, 'how fast time passes outside.'

'We should go back,' said Gobalt.

Yes! Alex thought. Go now, before Mum comes home.

'Or perhaps,' Olly said, 'you could go to another hill.'

The elves all went quiet and looked at her hard. Alex felt suspicious too. In fact, it was Alex who said, 'How do you mean?'

'Mean?' Olly said. 'Mean? How many things can "You could go to another hill" *mean*? I *mean*, darlings, that I know a hill whereon the wild thyme blows, while underneath the shaggy elves do dwell – apologies to Bill.'

'Who are you calling shaggy?' Runstrewel said.

'You know of another elf-hill?' Kernoggle said.

'It'll be empty and infested with big yins,' said Runstrewel. 'Like this one.'

'Give the lassie a hearing,' Dalgren said, and smiled at Olly again.

'I certainly think you should,' Olly said, 'because this hill I warble of isn't a bit like this one. It's chocka with elves! Hotching with 'em. And they've hardly noticed a thousand years going by – they're a bit out of the way, you see.'

'No kirks?' Kernoggle said, astonished.

'No ding-dongs?' said Gobalt.

'No,' Olly said, 'they've even got a few big yins with problems, being properly respectful and politely asking the elves for help.'

'No!' Kernoggle said.

'Oh, yes! I'm sure they'd welcome you.'

The elves looked at each other and shuffled in their seats. 'Not so sure of that,' Runstrewel said, and the others seemed to agree.

'There's no hiding it,' Kernoggle said, 'we're a quarrelsome lot, we elves.'

'The hill I'm talking about is at Halesdavy,' Olly said, 'but that's not what elves call it. Have you heard of Kenelmsfell?'

All four elves jerked up straight. 'Kenelmsfell?' Kernoggle said, and Runstrewel, holding his aching head said, 'Kenelmsfell's still there?'

'I'd have thought they'd have all cleared out a long time ago,' said Gobalt.

'Aye. Haven't the big yins built their brick

pens all over that hill?' Dalgren asked.

Olly leaned back comfortably in her chair. 'It's just one of those accidents of history. It's still countryside out that way, and the farmers haven't done much with the land. It's been rough pasture for . . . oh, I don't know how long, I'm just a townie. Centuries, I should think. There's no churches near, nobody much bothers to huff and puff all the way up there – there's nothing to see when you get to the top. So there the hill still is. Tell you what – shall I drop by and tell them all about you? I'll give it lots of the old hearts and flowers, I'll have 'em sobbing buckets over your sorry plight – and I'll ask if they'll think about letting you in there?'

The elves stared at her. Dalgren said, 'Would you do that for us?'

'Of course,' Olly said. 'Homing homeless elves, my speciality.'

'You are as kind as you are lovely,' Dalgren said.

'Oh la, sir! You make me blush!'

Alex was sitting up straight too. 'You know where there's an elf-hill, a real elf-hill?'

'I do believe that's what I was just saying, petal. But maybe not – I wasn't really listening.'

'Near here?'

'Over at Halesdavy, like I said. It's what . . . half an hour away? Maybe a bit more.'

'Can I come?' Alex said.

'I thought you weren't a witch?' Olly said.

'I'm not! But this is different. This is—'

'Let me go and see 'em on me own first,' Olly said, getting up from her chair. 'If they say yes, maybe you can tag along when I take the boys here over.'

Alex followed her out into the hall. 'That'd be great. I'd really like to see . . . would that be elf-land?'

'The hills are like an entrance into elf-land, yes. But, remember – they might say no.'

'And we'll be stuck with them.' Alex nodded towards the other room, where the elves were.

'They might be better behaved now,' Olly said as she let herself out. 'Now they've got hope.'

# 7. The Door in the Hill

Olly was right. Over the next couple of days, the elves weren't so bad. They didn't stuff themselves as much and then lie about all day complaining of feeling sick, although they still ate too many crisps and scattered the packets about and made a mess. And Kirsty had phoned to say she'd be home in two days.

The phone rang, and it was Olly. 'Little pal, little pal!' she cried, when Alex answered. 'I've been up to Halesdavy.'

'And?'

'The elves had a long powwow, and the upshot is . . . they'll let your mob in!'

Alex needed to make sure. 'So we're going to get rid of them?'

'That's what I said.'

'When can you take them away?'

'Well . . .' Olly said, considering.

'Oh, please make it tonight or tomorrow – please. Only Mum's coming back after that. I don't think she'll like these elves any better than she does ghosts or bogles.'

'Yeah, but little pal, Olly has things to do, people to—'

'Mum'll blame you,' Alex said. 'You know she always blames you when it's anything to do with magic or stuff like that.'

Olly went very quiet on the other end of the phone. Olly being quiet was unusual.

'You've never seen Mum *really* mad, have you?' Alex said.

'Er . . . I've seen her a bit miffed, and badly tetchy.'

'That's nothing,' Alex said.

'I dunno. I thought she was going to set the haggis on me.'

'Trust me, she can be a lot worse.'

'OK, all right, nuff said, little pal. Be ready tomorrow night.'

'What time?'

'Eleven.'

'What – at night?'

'Problem, petal?'

Olly never thought there was a problem about your parents letting you go out with a witch at eleven at night. 'I'll ask Dad . . .'

'Yeah. Ask him if he wants Kirsty to meet the elves.'

'He'll let me go,' Alex said.


The elves stood in the dark street, peering into the car through its open door. They'd never been in a car before.

'Good job I didn't bring Stormrider,' Olly said.

Alex didn't think much of the car either. It was the battered little Nova with differently coloured doors, that Olly borrowed from a friend when Stormrider, her big motorbike, wasn't suitable for the job in hand.

'Come on, chaps, let's be having you,' Olly said. 'Sooner you're aboard, sooner it'll be over.'

'How does it work?' Kernoggle asked.

'Big yin magic,' Olly said.

The elves seemed to find this comforting. After a little more muttering among themselves, they climbed into the back seat, scrambling past the folded-down front seat. Then Olly got in behind the wheel, and Alex climbed in beside her.

'Hold on tight!' Olly cried. 'Here we go!'

It was not a happy journey. The elves rolled about on the back seat, fell off into the foot well and yelled, demanding that the car be stopped.

'She told you to hold on tight,' Alex said.

'Make it stop, make it stop!' Kernoggle's little legs kicked at the floor of the car.

'Or we'll stop it!' Runstrewel said. He was clinging to a window handle.

'Do your worst!' Olly said. 'I don't think elf magic works on the internal combustion engine.'

They finally drew up at a field gateway in a dark country lane. Alex peered unhappily out into the darkness and couldn't see much more than his own reflection. It was as black out there as the inside of a black sack. And he was supposed to go wandering about in all that darkness, with no more protection than Olly and a bunch of elves. 'Is it far?' he asked, and heard the nervousness in his own voice.

'It is a bit of a trek,' Olly said, 'but it's me and the boys you should feel sorry for – you're young and thin with long legs.'

Alex got out of the car and tipped his seat forward so the elves could climb out.

'This way,' Olly said. She pointed a beam of light from her torch and marched off into the darkness. There was a stile into the field. Olly climbed over it, followed by Alex. The elves, struggling to keep up, squeezed between the bars of the gate beside the stile.

Olly led them up the hill, keeping close beside the hedge. It wasn't easy in the dark. Invisible branches kept slapping Alex across the face and poking him in the eye, and the ground underfoot was uneven, so he kept tripping and stumbling.

Even though they were going so slowly, the elves couldn't keep up at all. Olly and Alex repeatedly had to stop, in order to wait for them to catch up. Alex didn't like that, because it was chilly standing still, and also because it was easier to hear all the countryside noises. Stealthy rustling noises, like things creeping up on them; soft, breathy noises, like things standing nearby, trying to breathe quietly. Alex had to keep reminding himself that there were no bears or wolves in England any more. (Though perhaps just one or two had survived, unnoticed . . . and were waiting for their chance to eat him.)

Then the elves would come scrambling up, panting and complaining. 'Save your breath for the climb,' Olly said, and started off again.

At the end of a long, exasperating climb, they came out on a windy hilltop. Away in the distance were the bright lights of the town. To their other side, outlined in black against an almost black sky, was a round mound, topped with trees. The wind hissed through their leaves and branches with a sound like falling rain.

Olly stooped over, her hands on her knees. She panted for a bit, and then said, 'That's the hill. That's Kenelmsfell.'

Alex was too busy listening for the soft footfalls of wolves and bears to take much notice. The elves came straggling up.

'How much further?'

'Do you big yins have to walk so fast?'

'Olly says we're here,' Alex said.

The elves flopped down on the ground and blew out great puffs of air.

'Well, come on!' Olly said. 'We've got to go knock on the door.'

Alex followed her closer to the mound, and the elves heaved themselves up, groaning, and came too.

Alex was peering through the dark and continued to squint about him as they reached the foot of the mound. It was hard to see anything. 'Is there a *door*?'

'Not yet,' Olly said. She stamped on the ground – three stamps. 'By oak, by ash, by thorn! By Lok and Tod and Od.'

The hill opened.

# 8. Under the Hill

A great square door in the side of the mound swung inwards. From the hole came a cool, grey-blue, silvery light, like moonlight. The trees growing on the mound were lit, grey on black, by this cold light, and even tiny leaves and grass blades could be clearly seen. From

within the hole came, faintly, as if from far away, sounds of shouting, laughing and music.

Alex stood stock-still and stared. He couldn't move or speak.

The elves ambled past him, heading for the doorway in the hillside as if they were strolling into the local shop.

'Before we go in,' Olly said, 'a word of warning.'

'*Are* we going in?' Alex gasped.

'It'd be rude not to,' Olly said. 'Besides, we've come all this way. I could do with a sit-down – but *not* a cup of tea. That's what I wanted to tell you. While we're inside you mustn't eat or drink anything at all, under-stand? Not the teensiest little sip, not a crumb, nothing.'

'Why?' Alex asked. 'Will they try to poison us?'

'Why, no. It's just one of the laws – I was going to say 'laws of nature', but this is one of the unnatural laws of . . . well, unnature, I suppose. If you eat troll-bread, you become a troll, you see. If you eat elf-food, you become an elf, and you won't be able to come home.'

'What, even one crumb?' Alex said.

'Yes.'

'What, one little crumb will turn all of me into an elf? I'd think it'd take a couple of loaves at least.'

'Alex, petal—'

'And what about them? They've been stuffing their faces with our food, and they haven't turned into human beings, have they?'

'That's diff—'

'And they can still go back to elf-land – so why can't I eat their food and still go home?'

Olly sighed. 'Alex, my little flesh-eating microbe, witches have been hobnobbing with elves for centuries, and they all agree that it's a bad idea to eat elf-food or drink elf-drink, so . . . '

'Has a proper test ever been done?' Alex

said. 'With a large sample and control groups?'

Olly sighed again. 'I doubt it, oh blight of my life. Are we going to stand out here arguing all night, or are we going in? And *please* don't try any experiments with the food and drink. I think it's all made out of bones, worms and dead leaves anyway, whatever it looks like.'

Alex thought he would prefer to stand around talking rather than go into that hole in the ground. But Olly was heading for the hole, and if he wasn't careful he'd be left outside, alone, in the dark, with the wolves and bears. He ran after her. Better get inside fast, before he had time to think about it.

The door in the hillside opened into a short, stone-lined tunnel, with rutted, stony earth underfoot. The silvery light was coming from a wooden door at the other end. Alex followed Olly through it and heard the door shut behind him.

He turned to look at the closed door. It was made of great heavy planks studded with big nail-heads and had massive, fancy hinges. Two elves were just slotting a bar into place.

Nervously, Alex turned to see what was in front of him.

It was a long, high room, the walls hidden by lengths of cloth covered in bright embroidery, which waved slightly in the draughts. From one end of the room to the other burned a fire, with cauldrons suspended over it at intervals. From those cauldrons came steam, and pleasant smells.

There were tables, too, on either side of the fire, and elves everywhere – elves at the tables, eating and drinking; elves sitting on benches against the walls; elves walking about, elves playing harps, elves singing.

There was an elf holding a bone and playing tug of war with a wonderful little dog that was all white except for its red ears. Alex would have liked to take that dog home with him.

Kernoggle, Runstrewel, Gobalt and Dalgren were staring about them with their mouths open.

'Now this is something *like*!' Runstrewel said.

'Just like the old days!' said Kernoggle.

'Come on and meet the king of the hill,' Olly said, and led the way forward, walking beside the fire and in front of one line of tables. The four elves followed her. Alex did too, thinking: a *king*? Of a *hill*? It seemed pretty daft to call yourself the king of a hill.

The fires were hot as he passed them, and the noise of chatter and cups banging on tables and dogs barking made his ears hurt. His feet skittered through dry rushes and bones on the hard floor, and smoke irritated his throat and nose and made his eyes water. The elves at the tables paused in their talk and stared at each of them as they went past.

At the end of the long room was a platform, and on it stood a table set crossways. It was there that the elf-king of the hill sat. He was old, even for an elf, and wrapped in furs. On his head was a delicate diadem of golden leaves. A gold cup was before him, and to his right and left sat tiny, beautiful elf-ladies. Alex kept looking at them, wondering, were they his wives, daughters, sisters?

'Evening, Your Maj,' Olly said, sitting down on the edge of the platform. Elf-dogs immediately scrambled about her, wagging

71

their tails, hoisting their red ears and putting their forepaws on her knees. 'I've brought those lost elves I was telling you about.'

Runstrewel, Kernoggle, Dalgren and Gobalt all lined up in front of the platform, taking off their hats and trying to look like the sort of respectable elves that a king would want in his hill.

But the king was looking at Alex. 'Who is the young witch?' he asked.

'Oh, this is my little pal, Alex. He keeps telling everyone he isn't a witch.'

The elf-king laughed, and the beautiful elf-ladies stared, and Alex felt quite angry with Olly.

'If I take you into my hill,' the king said to the four elves standing in a row, 'will you swear loyalty to me?'

All four of them nodded eagerly. 'Be sure we will, King,' said Kernoggle.

'You will keep my laws, fight for me, work for me?'

'We will, we will,' the four of them agreed.

'Then find yourselves places, and eat,' said the king.

Grinning, the four elves turned and hurried off into the crowd. 'Elf-beer!' Runstrewel said to Alex as he went, while Dalgren winked and said, 'Women!'

All four of them disappeared among the crowded tables, and Alex turned back to Olly and the king. 'I won't be so rude, Olivia,' said the king, 'as to offer you or your friend anything to eat or drink.'

'We know you would feed us generously, if we could accept,' Olly said. 'And we thank you for the thought.'

'Will you stay a while and be entertained?' the king asked.

Olly looked at Alex. 'It is late . . .'

'But when you leave our hill,' said the king, 'it will be no more than one eye-blink after you came in, no matter how long you stay.'

One of the beautiful elf-ladies leaned

forward. 'Do stay a while. Friends should be in no hurry to part.'

Alex nudged Olly. 'Go on, let's stay – *Olivia*.'

Olly looked down at him. 'Oh, all right, then, Alexander *Bertram*.'

Alex's mouth fell open. How did Olly know his full name – the name he kept most secret? Well – she was a witch.

Olly made a slight bow to the king. 'King – ladies – Alex and I thank you, and would be glad to stay awhile.

It was impossible to say how long they stayed. Sometimes it seemed to Alex like a few minutes, barely enough time to take a look around. Sometimes it seemed like several hours, or even days, too long. At times it seemed to pass very, very slowly, so he had time to examine the pictures on the wall-hangings and the thick bands of embroidery on the king's tablecloth and at other times to whizz past in a blur, so he could hardly remember anything.

There were dancers, and singing – he remembered that, though he couldn't remember the music or any of the words. There had been juggling and a display of sword-fighting, during which the elves stamped, whistled and yelled deafeningly. At some point he noticed that the long hall was lit by what seemed to be a single great pearl, hanging from the ceiling, glowing softly. That was what had made the silvery light that had spilled from the open hill. He stared at it for a long, long time.

'Don't get lost,' Olly said to him. 'Time to leave, I think.' And she took him by the arm and they walked out, through all the elves, who took no notice of them, as if they were ghosts. The hill opened, and they were in the chilly, damp air, with a smell of earth and grass, washed over by the silvery light of the pearl that hung in the hill.

Then the hill closed, and they were on the dark, cold hillside.

# 9. A Few Friends

A key turned in the lock, and Kirsty shouted, 'I'm back! Get the kettle on! Come and give me a kiss. Where are my slaves to carry the bags?'

Alex came running down the stairs from his room, and Rob came out of the kitchen. Rob hugged Kirsty, and she put her arms round his neck.

'Good to have you back – I missed you.'

'Good to be back. Where's Alex?'

'Here!'

Kirsty stretched out an arm and drew Alex into the hug. Alex put his arms round her, surprised how glad he was that she was home.

'Everybody all right?' Rob asked.

'They're all the same. Have you two been OK?'

'We've been fine – haven't we, Alex?'

'Oh, fine, Dad.' He and his dad looked at each other, thinking, Thank goodness we got rid of the gnomes. She'll never know, because we'll never tell her.

'I'll get your bags,' Rob said, and went out to the car.

'I'll put the kettle on.' Alex went into the kitchen.

Kirsty followed him. 'You have been good!'

Alex looked around. The kitchen wasn't particularly tidy, but Kirsty wasn't unreasonable like that. She didn't expect every single packet to be put away or every cup, dish and spoon to be washed.

'We've been brilliant!' Alex said. He saw Rob coming in at the front door and called, 'There're no crumbs on the floor, are there, Dad, and no crisp packets down the chairs.'

'Of course not,' Rob said. 'As if we'd do

things like that.'

'You're a treasure, and you're a wee gem,' Kirsty said. 'I shall be on the sofa with my feet up. Bring me tea and chocolate.'

'Yea, oh mistress,' Rob said.

'Yea, mighty one,' Alex said, and he and his dad grinned at each other. They really were glad to have Kirsty back.

'We got away with it,' Alex whispered, and Rob nodded.

They carried on thinking they'd got away with it for all of a week. Everything was grand. Kirsty was happy to be home and full of good humour, calling them gems and treasures all the time. Rob and Alex basked in it.

And then came the night when Alex, asleep in his bed, was startled awake by cries of, 'Rob! Rob! Rob-ert!' It was Kirsty, yelling, downstairs.

Oh, no, Alex thought. What now? Boggarts? Ghosts? Kows? Or was it only burglars?

Feet pounded on the stairs as his mother

ran up them. 'Alex! Rob! Get up! Get up now!'

Alex, in his pyjama bottoms, rolled out of bed and stumbled to his door. On the landing stood his mum, in a long T-shirt, and his dad, in boxer shorts and socks. It reminded Alex of when Hairy Bill, the bogle, had frightened Kirsty in the middle of the night. And then

there was the time when the Green Lady and the White Lady had been chased out of their new home by the Sulky Smudge and had come to scream around Alex's bed.

And now here they were again, in their nightclothes, yelling on the landing.

Honestly, Alex thought, it was getting to be a family tradition.

'Wassma'er now?' Rob said.

'Hairy men!' Kirsty said. 'Hundreds of hairy little men! Everywhere!'

'Hairy men?' Rob said.

'I went across the landing to the bathroom,' Kirsty said, 'and I heard the telly going. I thought you'd left it on, so I went down to turn it off, and . . . hairy little men! Everywhere! Garden gnomes! Alex, what do you know about this?'

Alex sighed deeply. He might have known the peace of the last week was too good to be true. 'They're not garden gnomes. They're elves.'

'Aha!' Kirsty said. 'So you *do* know something about them! I knew it!'

A voice from the bottom of the stairs called, 'Rob? It's all right, mate.'

Rob switched on the landing light and looked over the banister. Alex looked round the end of it. At the bottom of the stairs, looking up, stood Runstrewel, Kernoggle and Gobalt.

'It's only us,' Runstrewel said.

'With a few friends,' Kernoggle added.

'Nothing to worry about, mate.'

'Nothing to . . . !' Kirsty threw her arms in the air. 'So you're in on it, too!' she cried, jabbing Rob in the chest with a finger. 'And that Olly Spellmaker, I bet! What are they doing infesting *my* house and not hers? I want them out! *Out!*'

'They're not ghosts, Mum,' Alex said. 'Or house-spirits.'

'More sort of garden-spirits, as I understand it,' Rob said. 'Good for the roses.'

82

Kirsty raised her arms to the ceiling. 'I don't care! I want them out! I am not running a holiday camp for spooks! Get rid of them!'

Rob groaned and started down the stairs. Alex grabbed his pyjama top and followed him.

'I hope we're not causing trouble with your good lady,' Kernoggle said, as they reached the foot of the stairs.

'You are,' Rob said, and headed along the hall towards the living room.

'She frightened the life out of *us*,' Runstrewel said, following. 'She let out such a yell, we thought she was a banshee. And we were only having a bit of a laugh.'

Rob stopped outside the living room. 'I don't know what you're doing here at all!'

'Yeah!' Alex said. 'You moved out to Kenelmsfell! What are you doing back here?'

'Just visiting,' Kernoggle said. 'You know – dropping in on old friends.'

Rob pushed open the living-room door and went in. He said, 'I don't believe . . . !'

Alex quickly ducked into the room behind his father. His mouth opened, but he just gasped.

The sofa was crammed with elves. They were sitting on top of each other. Some of them were elf-women.

In each armchair there were four or five elves, and more were sitting on the floor. The coffee table was covered with cans of drink with straws in, bags of crisps and nuts, bananas and tangerines and an open box of small cakes. The television was on, showing lots of people running about with guns.

'What's all this?' Rob demanded.

'Well, see, it's like this, mate . . .' Runstrewel started.

'We just invited a few friends round to see the place,' Kernoggle said.

'A few friends!'

'It isn't your place!' Alex said.

'Yes, it is!' said Runstrewel. 'Our ancestral place – remember?'

'But it's not your sofa,' Alex said. 'Or your telly. Or your food – or anything!'

A sudden blast of music made them jump and look round. Some of the elves had started the CD player, and were jumping around and dancing.

'Turn that off!' Rob yelled. 'It's three in the morning!'

The elves who were watching television agreed. They jumped off the sofa and ran across the room to demand that the CD be turned off. An argument started, and then a brawl.

'Cut it out!' Rob said, going across to break up the fight.

'You'd all moved out to Kenelmsfell!' Alex said. 'We thought you were happy there.'

'Aye, well, yes, we were . . .' Kernoggle said.

'Aye, but they've no television,' Runstrewel said.

'Benches, not sofas,' said Dalgren, emerging from the crowd. 'No crisps, no chocolate.'

'We told everybody about this place,' Runstrewel said, 'and they wanted to see it for themselves.'

Rob gave a roar. Alex looked round and saw his dad hobbling towards him. 'They kicked me and *bit* me!'

Alex followed his dad into the hall then Rob went upstairs and into the bathroom to wash his hand. 'How can I tell the doctor I was bitten by a savage garden gnome?'

Alex was leaning in the doorway of the bathroom, but heard a noise from his parents' bedroom. He went and looked round the door. Kirsty, fully dressed, was packing a suitcase.

'Mum! What are you doing?'

'Packing.'

'But why?'

'I'm going to a hotel. I'm not staying here with this bedlam.'

'But, Mum . . . !'

She put on her coat. 'I'm going. Boggarts, ghosts – now garden gnomes. I'm not putting up with it.' She picked up her case and walked past him. 'I'll let you know where I am. You can let me know when you get rid of *them*.'

As she passed the bathroom and started down the stairs, Rob spun round. 'Kirsty! Where are you going?'

Kirsty called back, 'Goodbye!'

From downstairs, the sound of the television competed with the music from the CD player. Rob sat down on the edge of the bath.

'She's gone to a hotel until we get rid of the elves,' Alex explained.

Rob stood up. 'Phone Olly.'

'But it's the middle of the night, Dad!'

From downstairs came gunfire and guitar solos.

'PHONE OLLY!'

# 10. 'Out! Out! Out!'

The phone rang six times and then went to answerphone. Alex redialled. Four tries later, the phone at the other end was picked up and Olly's voice, more bleary and irritable than Alex had ever heard it, said, 'Hello!'

'Olly!'

'*Alex?*' she said, sounding annoyed. She'd never been annoyed with him before. It was unnerving. 'It's . . . what? . . . three-thirty, *pal*.'

'But, Olly—'

'Alex, this *has* to wait.'

Rob took the phone from Alex, and said into it, 'Olly, you get your big bum round here *now*. The garden gnomes are back – hundreds of 'em – and my wife's left me. You come and sort this out, or I'll be leading a mob with burning torches and pitchforks round to your place, no kidding.' He ended the call.

'*Dad!* You can't talk to Olly like that.'

'I just did.'

'She'll turn you into a frog.'

'Right now I'd be a lot happier as a frog. I wish I'd been born a frog. What do frogs know or care?'

Alex didn't like it when his dad was angry, so he went away to his bedroom to be by himself. But there were elves in there, sitting on his bed, playing his computer games, cheering and hooting. They broke off and stared at him crossly, and Alex didn't feel up to arguing with garden gnomes. 'Excuse *me*,' he said and went to sit on the bottom stair to wait for Olly.

Olly didn't come. The elves got noisier and more insufferable, but still Olly didn't come.

There was less and less room to sit on the

stairs, because elves kept coming to sit there, to talk, and eat crisps. Some of them got together in groups and sang, which would have been pleasant, except that they were all singing different songs. There were elves with little fiddles and pipes, playing away, and even a couple with bagpipes. Kirsty had always said that bagpipes sounded like 'a cat being ironed', and now Alex could hear for himself how true that was.

More elves were coming and going from the kitchen and living room. The sounds of music and film soundtracks shook the walls.

From upstairs on the landing, Rob shouted, 'You dirty little . . . !'

'What's up?' Alex yelled above the din.

Rob looked over the landing. 'One of the little swine has been sick on the landing! Why should I have to clean up after piggish elves? It was bad enough having to clean up after you as a baby!'

The doorbell rang. Alex got up from the

stairs and opened the front door. There stood Mr Abbey from next door, dressed in a duffel coat, pyjama trousers and trainers. 'Do you know what time it is?' Mr Abbey demanded.

'Er . . . Dad!'

Rob came running down the stairs.

'The noise!' Mr Abbey shouted. He didn't seem to see the elves, though they were teeming up and down the hall and stairs. 'What are you playing at, having a party at this time in the morning?'

'I'm not . . .' Rob began. 'Um . . . I'm sorry. I'll try to get the noise down.'

'You'd better!' Mr Abbey shouted, and turned and strode off down the path.

'Hear! hear!' someone else shouted from across the street. Another neighbour was leaning out of a bedroom window.

Rob shut the door rather harder than he needed to.

'I know,' Alex said, 'why don't we pull the plugs?'

'I did,' Rob said. 'They put them in again.'

'Take the fuses out!'

'Can't find me screwdriver,' Rob said. 'Kirsty had it for something and I don't know what she's done with it.'

There was a rush of elves across the landing upstairs, sounding like a charge of elephants, followed by a roaring cheer. The light-fitting shook. And still Olly didn't come.

At four in the morning they had a phone call from another neighbour asking them, for God's sake, to pack it in. Half an hour later, the police knocked at the door. 'We've had complaints from your neighbours, sir. About the noise. Could you keep it down, please, sir?'

Rob sighed. 'I'll do my best.'

'Thank you, sir.'

Closing the door, Rob said, 'Where is Olly?'

'You were rude to her,' Alex said.

'She's not going to hold that against us, is she?'

'You said her bum was big.'

But Rob wasn't listening. He was looking past Alex with an expression of some alarm.

Alex turned.

Behind him, elves were filling the hall. Elves were crowded on the stairs. They looked angry, and they'd gone quiet.

Then they started to chant. 'Out! Out! Out! Out!'

All the elves started to come towards them, and some were waving shovels and pickaxe handles. Alex quickly backed down the hall until he was against the front door, with his dad.

'Out! Out! Out!'

The elves were small, but there were so many of them; and they were very strong. Rob pushed Alex hard against the door and stood

in front of him. 'Now look here . . .' he started.

Alex thought, Oh, Dad. They aren't going to listen.

The elves rushed them. They were all round them, and they were pulling at Rob's jeans and kicking him, yelling, punching. They were shouting, 'Get 'em! Scrag 'em!'

Rob was struggling and shouting, trying to kick his legs free, but crying out in pain as much as anger.

This is no good, Alex thought. Dad's going to be hurt. Bitten. Could a mad elf give you rabies?

Alex wriggled round and twisted the door knob. But there were elves leaning against the door and he couldn't open it.

'Dad! Help me . . . get the door open!'

'Marmalize 'em, pummel 'em!' chanted the elves.

'We've got to get out, Dad!'

Rob kicked and shoved a great heap of elves away. He wrenched open the front door, and he and Alex fell out on to the path and lawn, and a heap of elves fell out with them.

The elves jumped up and ran back to the house. They danced on the doorstep and laughed and chanted, 'Ours! Ours! Ours!' Then they slammed the door shut.

Alex and Rob sat on the front lawn in the early grey chill.

'Our house!' Rob said.

The letter box flapped and a voice from

inside yelled. '*Our* house! Our ancestral hill! Our land!'

Elves appeared at the window, pointing at them and pulling faces. 'Our telly!' came the little voices from behind the glass. 'Our CDs! Our radiators!'

Alex looked at his dad. 'Mum's going to *love* this.'

It was then that Olly rode up on Stormrider.

# 11. Fire!

The noise of Stormrider's engine reverberated between the brick walls of the street; the early morning light shone on its chrome-work and on Olly's helmet and black leathers. Alex, cold, tired and hungry, thought he'd never seen such a beautiful sight. Oh, heroic Olly!

Both he and Rob scrambled up from the lawn and ran out of the gate. 'Oh, Olly, I'm glad to see you!' Alex said.

'They've thrown us out of the house!' Rob said.

'What are we going to do? Where have you been?'

'We called you ages ago!'

Olly, sitting on Stormrider, pulled off her

helmet. She smiled at them. 'Tell me, Rob – does my bum look big in this?'

'Oh, Olly, I'm sorry,' Rob said. 'I lost my cool . . . I said things I didn't mean . . .'

'"Get your big bum round here," I think were your *exact* words—'

'I'm sorry, Olly!'

'And there were some threats, I seem to recall,' Olly said, 'along the lines of, if I didn't get my *big bum* round here, you would come with torches and pitchforks to sort me out.'

Alex nudged Rob hard in the side. '*Dad*, I told you.'

'Olly, what can I say?'

'Little man, little man,' Olly said, 'threats are not things to use against witches.'

'Olly, please,' Rob said. 'For God's sake – or the goddess's or whatever . . . My wife's left me, my son's out on the street, my house is being squatted by a revolting pack of garden gnomes! OK, I spoke out of turn, but I'm under *stress* here! Help!'

'Olly, please help,' Alex said.

'Darlings, of course I'm going to help,' Olly said. She got off her bike and opened the luggage compartment. 'Here, I think this will sort things out.' She took out a box about the size of Alex's lunch box. 'There you are.'

They looked at the box. It was neatly made of wood, with shining metal hinges. Its sides were carved with pictures of deer. Altogether, a very nice box. But it wasn't very big, and it was hard to imagine how it could be of any use.

'What's in it?' Alex asked. 'A bomb?'

'As if I would go about with bombs! A respectable witch like me!'

'A gun?' Alex asked.

'A gun! Honestly, you play too many computer games. Be sensible. It is, of course, full of soldiers.'

'Soldiers!' Alex and Rob said together, and stared at the box again.

'You couldn't fit even one soldier in that,'

101

Alex said. 'Not even his foot.'

'*Elf*-soldiers, you pudding,' Olly said.

Alex thought of the elves in the house. 'You couldn't fit even one of them in there!'

'I assure you,' Olly said, 'that there's a whole regiment in there. Even two or three regiments – I never was sure how many a regiment was. *Anyway!* Enough of this chitting and chatting.' Taking the box with her, Olly strode up the path to the front door. Alex and Rob followed her.

At the doorstep, Olly unfastened the clasps that held the box shut. 'Rob, open the door, please.'

'How? With what?' Rob asked. 'Olly, I'm in my boxers.'

Olly looked surprised, as if she hadn't noticed. She put the box down on the step and took off her jacket. 'Darling! Have my coat! You must be freezing.'

'Thank you.'

Alex thought his dad looked a sight, in bare

legs, boxer shorts and Olly's leather jacket. 'How about me?'

'You do at least have a pyjama jacket between you and the hostile elements,' Olly said. 'But how are we to introduce the box of soldiers to the enemy? Throw it in through a window?'

'No!' Rob said.

'There's the cat flap,' Alex said. 'It's how the gnomes got in to start with.'

'Ideal!' Olly said. 'And also peachy-dory and hunky-keen.' She led the way round the side of the house.

Alex and Rob stood beside her as she bent over and pushed the box through the cat flap. They could see that Olly's bum did, indeed, look big in her motorcycle leathers. The cat flap clonked shut, and Olly straightened.

They waited, looking at each other. After a few seconds, a sound came from the other side of the door. Hundreds of little voices, chanting, 'Hup! Hup! Hup! Hup!'

Alex fell to his hands and knees, lifted the cat flap and peered in. From the open box was pouring a swarm of creatures, small as flies, small as bees. They grew bigger as they got further from the box, bigger and bigger, until they reached elf-size, and formed up into lines. They wore helmets and breastplates and carried spears.

And then, from the box, came strange things. Alex couldn't think what they were at first, but as they grew bigger he realized that they were dragons. Small dragons, with writhing tails and puffs of grey smoke coming from their nostrils – and elves in helmets riding on their backs!

He felt his head might pop with astonishment if he looked any longer, and so he pulled

back from the cat flap. 'Olly, where did you get that box?'

'From the king under the hill,' Olly said.

'What – at Kenelmsfell?'

'That's the chap. "Here, Ol," he said, "shove a dose of this-here up their kilts. That'll sort 'em out."'

Alex couldn't resist looking through the cat flap again. The elves on dragon-back were

leading off into the hall, and the foot-elves were running after them. From the direction of the living room came thumps, wallops and squeals, cries of, 'Geroff!' and bangs, crashes and yells.

Alex heard noises close beside him and jumped with alarm – but it was just his dad and Olly moving away from him. Scrambling to his feet, he went after them.

They were in the backyard, leaning their arms comfortably on the window sill and looking in through the window. Alex joined them.

Inside was a blur of movement. Elves were scattering everywhere as the elves on dragon-back charged. They ran under the coffee table, but the foot-elves ran after them and drove them out on to the rug as the dragon-elves came charging round the armchair. A spurt of flame from a dragon neatly lit the wick of a candle that Kirsty kept on the hearth.

Elves clambered up on to the settee, but the

dragons leaped right after them, with flames flickering from their nostrils.

'They'll set the house on fire!' Rob cried.

'Oh, don't be such a worry-wart,' Olly said. 'I bet you've got insurance.'

'Oh, yeah.' Rob was fidgeting as he watched the goings-on in his living room. 'Dear Insurance Company, I'd like to make a claim because my house was invaded by garden gnomes and burned to the ground by mini-dragons.'

'Oh, they'll be very careful,' Olly said.

Just as she said this, two of the dragons opened their wings and took to the air, swooped round the light fitting and dived, rapidly spitting out little balls of fire at the surging elves below – who ran about, ducking, with hands over their heads. Alex saw Gobalt with his beard on fire, until a lady-elf emptied a can of drink over him to put it out. A dragon landed near them, with an elf on its back, and the lady-elf, in a temper, ran at it and slapped its nose. Alex winced, thinking the dragon would breathe fire all over her but, instead, the dragon neatly knocked her down and put one clawed foot on her back. Its rider pointed at Gobalt with a stick and Gobalt lay down on his belly and clasped his hands behind his head.

'The rug, the rug!' Rob said, doing a little dance and pointing.

The rug was smouldering, where a dragon's spit-ball had landed. Another spit-ball hit the mirror above the mantelpiece, with a lovely flash of reflected light, and then a crack they heard even outside, as the mirror broke.

But the rushing about on the floor was growing less. In a very few moments, the elf-soldiers were the only ones left standing. All the others were lying on the floor.

The flying dragons landed on the backs of the armchairs before rising into the air again and flying off into the hall. Some of the elf-soldiers followed.

'Is this legal?' Rob said. 'What about elf-rights?'

'I didn't think you'd be worried too much about *their* rights,' Olly said, 'after they took over your house.'

'I'm just scared that, after all this, I'm going to get sued by elves,' Rob said.

The elf-soldiers that had gone into the hall came back, bringing one or two other elves with them as prisoners.

'I think,' Olly said, 'that we might be able to talk to your visitors now. Shall we try?'

# 12. Arrest

Elf-soldiers opened the door to them, and one fierce-looking elf saluted Olly. 'All under control, ma'am!'

'Very good, sergeant,' Olly said. 'We'll carry on.'

She led Rob and Alex into the sitting room and sat down on the sofa, among the mess the elves had made.

There were still crowds of elves in the room, but the soldier-elves had carried in the box in which they had travelled and were herding the troublemaking elves towards it. As they neared the box, they grew smaller and smaller, shrinking to the size of flies.

Olly, sitting in state on the sofa, said, 'I'd

like to talk to . . . to . . . *who* are they, Alex?'

'Runstrewel and Kernoggle,' he said, 'and Gobalt and Dalgren.'

'Those are they.' Olly turned to the elf-sergeant. 'Where are they?'

'Step forward,' bellowed the sergeant, 'you *horrible* elves!'

Runstrewel and Kernoggle, Gobalt and Dalgren shuffled forward from against the wall. They looked . . . rumpled. And singed. Runstrewel had a bloody nose, and Dalgren a swollen, reddened eye that was going to turn black. Gobalt's beard was burned to a frazzle.

'Stand up straight!' the sergeant yelled. 'Answer Madam Witch when she questions you! Speak up, speak clear!'

Olly looked them over. Runstrewel stared back, still ready for a fight. Kernoggle looked embarrassed, Gobalt scared and, Dalgren, if anything, rather amused.

'*Why?*' Olly said, at last. 'Didn't I go to the king of Kenelmsfell and ask him to take you in, as a favour? Didn't you say that Kenelmsfell was what you wanted?'

'It is, indeed, a very fine place,' Kernoggle said.

'It's very good,' Runstrewel said. 'Grand. Real elf.'

'But you're not there,' Olly said. 'You're here. Making yourself a flaming nuisance. And a flamed one, by the look of you.'

'Well,' Dalgren said, 'Kenelmsfell's fine. But it's slow.'

'*Yeah!*' Gobalt agreed.

'So, let me get this straight,' Olly said. 'You want a real old traditional, down-home elf-hill, with food like momma used to make – but with televisions and computer games as well.'

'Yeah!' Gobalt said.

'Well, not here!' Rob said.

Olly sighed. 'Take 'em away, sergeant.'

'Right you are, ma'am,' said the sergeant, and the remaining elves were quickly packed away into their box, followed by the dragons, who had been cooling off in a corner. The sergeant was the last one in. Alex watched as he vaulted over the box's side, shrinking in the air. The box lid was pulled shut by an arm that reached up from inside.

'Right,' Olly said. She got up and lifted the box, tucking it under her arm. 'Better get this back to the king.'

'They're only going to come back again, aren't they?' Alex said, and his dad looked glum.

'They might not,' Olly said.

'They will,' Alex said. He knew how hard it was to give up computer games. 'Mum'll leave for good if they do.'

# 13. Buying a Present

'Have they gone?' Kirsty asked. 'Really gone?'

'Would we lie to you?' Alex asked.

'All the time.' Kirsty opened the front door and peered into the hall. Since that appeared to be free of gnomes, she edged inside and checked the kitchen and living room. 'And you haven't moved in other ghosties or ghoulies *of any kind*?'

'Not a one,' Alex said. 'Not an imp, nor a skrike or even a clabbernabber.'

'Nothing witch-related, or supernatural, or not of this world?'

'The house is paranormal-free, we promise,' Rob said, hand on heart.

Kirsty marched into the living room. 'The

rug! The rug's scorched! And the armchair – the curtains! Look at these scorch marks! What have you been doing?'

'The mirror's broken too,' Alex said. He felt that they might as well confess everything and get it over with.

Kirsty put her hands on her hips and glared.

'Well,' Rob said, 'see, there were these little dragons . . .'

'Dragons? Where? I thought you said . . . ?'

'They've gone, Mum. They came with the soldier-elves to round up the other elves, and a few things got . . . a bit singed.'

'But they've gone now!' Rob said. 'And they won't be coming back!'

Kirsty looked round suspiciously. 'Are you sure?'

'Sure!' Rob and Alex said together.

Kirsty threw herself on the sofa. 'I shall have something to say about this later! But, for now – make me tea!'

Alex went to make the tea, wondering how long it would be before the elves came back. He was sure they would. They'd come back once, hadn't they? Next time, they'd probably bring the king with them.

As he carried the tea in to Kirsty, he found himself glancing at the cat flap. A shifting patch of sunlight in the hallway caught his eye – was that a marauding elf? Even in the living room he sent quick looks into all the corners. It was going to be difficult, living in constant expectation of elves.

It was more than a week – an anxious but thankfully elf-free week – before Olly phoned. 'Little pal! Do you want to come and visit your old friends, the elves?'

'I've had enough of elves to last me a lifetime!'

'Don't you want to come and see why they won't ever bother you again, thanks to clever old *me*?'

'They won't ever bother us again?' Alex said.

'They won't need to. They couldn't be happier. Want to know why?'

'You've moved them into some other poor beggar's house?'

'No.'

'They've moved in with you? – No, not even elves could live happily with you.'

'Charmed, darling. Why don't you come and see? Pick you up in an hour?'

'On Stormrider?'

'I'll bring you a helmet.'

'Mum'll go mad.'

'What she doesn't know, little pal, won't affect her mental balance.'

Riding on the back of Stormrider was as frightening as it was exhilarating. It was especially scary to think that your life was in the hands of someone as daffy as Olly. Alex gritted his teeth, hung on as tightly as he could and leaned with the bike as they went round

corners. And finally Stormrider roared through the gate and pulled up outside . . .

'A garden centre?'

Olly pulled off her helmet, setting her dragon earrings bobbing. 'Yes, Alex, little mate, it came to me while I was contemplating me herbaceous. You come on in and see.'

They went through a wide door into a wider hall, where there were shelves of gardening books, racks of seeds, displays of pots and stacks of plastic sacks of compost. More doors led into a yard, where Alex could see aisles of trees and flowers.

'But this is just a *garden centre*.'

'Oh, how little faith!' Olly said. 'This way.'

She led the way past bird baths and bird tables, wind chimes and small Grecian goddesses to a coffee shop. And off the coffee shop was a television room, where people sat watching videos of gardening programmes, with computers, where they could play computer games or replan their garden.

Next to the coffee shop was a model village. Five little houses with thatched roofs were clustered round a village green, which had a real duck pond. Real ducks swam in the pond – they looked enormous against the little houses – and occasionally got out and waddled outside to the ponds in the gardens.

Besides the five houses, there was a model 'Village Shoppe', and a model village pub, called the Little Jug. It had tables and benches outside. On the backcloth was painted the spire of the village church, poking up from among trees and, beyond that, hills and sky.

Alex gazed at this scene, wondering why Olly had brought him to see it and what it had to do with the el—

'Oh, no,' he said.

'Yep,' said Olly. 'Isn't it cute? At Christmas, they pile it all over with fake snow, and have carols playing from the church.'

Alex was looking round. 'Where are they?'

'Who knows? Sleeping it off, probably. Or maybe they're passing themselves off as plastic gnomes in "Garden Ornaments".'

Alex was studying the little thatched houses. 'They don't live in them – do they?'

'They're . . . er . . . making them over,' Olly said. 'They're handy little so-and-sos. They're digging down to make 'em larger – reinforcing, of course – putting in water and lighting, building furniture – they use wood from the decking-and-trellis section. Of course, they don't really need heating or kitchens.'

121

Alex stepped over the rail that separated the public from the model village, and was about to tap at one of the doors, when Olly said, 'Come away, come away – don't attract attention like that.'

Alex looked round. Olly was moving away, looking back at him and jerking her head to tell him to follow, making her earrings bob. He stepped back over the rail and she led him outside, where there was a damp, chilly wind blowing. They wandered through shelves of potted plants to an area displaying statues, urns and pillars. A platform held several shelves of garden gnomes. They were dressed very like the elves, and Alex and Olly studied each one carefully, whether they were pushing wheelbarrows, shouldering picks, fishing or mooning, but they were just ordinary garden gnomes.

A particularly chilly breeze blew past them, and Alex shivered.

'It is a bit taters out here,' Olly said. 'I bet I know where they are.'

They went back inside, to the television room. They stood at the back, looking round, while three people watched the video. 'Aha,' Olly said, and nodded.

There was a shelf at the side of the room holding vases of flowers and pot-plants. Among these plants were four gnomes – model gnomes, plastic gnomes, you might think – sitting, lying and lounging. As Alex looked, he saw one of the gnomes scratch its nose. It was Dalgren.

Alex and Olly crossed the room and leaned against the shelf, as if they were just going to watch the screen for a while.

'Hello, lads,' Olly said. 'Settling in?'

'Oh, aye,' Runstrewel said. He was also lying on his side, propping his head up on one hand. ''S great. Couldn't be better.'

'Good idea of yours, Olly,' Kernoggle said. He was leaning his back against the wall, smoking a long pipe.

'Don't people *see* you?' Alex asked.

'They see garden gnomes,' Kernoggle said. 'That's what they expect to see, so they take no notice.'

'If they see us move,' Dalgren said, folding his arms, 'they think it's a trick of the light.'

'They rub their eyes and forget about it,' Kernoggle said.

Runstrewel got up, walked across to Alex and punched him on the arm. Alex looked round wildly, but no one had noticed.

'Don't worry, bairn,' Runstrewel said.

'We've got everything we want here. We won't be coming back to yours.'

'Nor to Kenelmsfell, neither,' Gobalt said.

'*Everything's* here!' Dalgren said, getting up and strolling over to join them. Alex looked round again, but still no one had noticed.

'There's crisps and nuts and chocolates,' said Dalgren.

'And fizzy drinks,' said Kernoggle.

'Coffee,' said Runstrewel.

'Computers.'

'Trees.'

'Fruit.'

'Vegetables.'

'Television.'

'Couldn't be better,' Runstrewel said.

'Madam Witch,' said Kernoggle, 'we owe you thanks.'

'Oh, never mention it,' Olly said.

'All right,' said Runstrewel, turning his back and walking away, 'we won't.'

'Never mind him, Madam Witch,' Kernoggle said, and Gobalt and Dalgren nodded. 'If ever you need our help, be sure to call on us.'

'You too, wee un,' said Dalgren.

'Thank you,' Olly said. 'I'm sure we'll be keeping in touch. Shall we go for a coffee, little pal?'

As they queued to buy their coffee, Olly said to the girl behind the counter, 'Tell me, sweetie, have you *seen* anything here?'

The girl, handing her a cup of coffee, looked at her blankly.

'I'm psychic, you see,' Olly said. 'Matter of fact, I'm a witch.' Alex turned his back on them. He was so embarrassed he wanted to run away and hide. 'And I get a *feeling* about this place . . .'

The girl continued to stare blankly, but an older woman turned from stacking fresh cups. 'Funny you should say that . . . cos there have been some funny things going on . . .'

'Oh?' Olly said, on an interested note.

'Things going missing out of stock.'

'Crisps,' said the girl.

'The television being on when we come in first thing . . .'

'Footsteps,' said the girl.

'Yeah . . . We're starting to think the place is haunted.'

'Oh, not haunted,' Olly said. 'Well, not in a bad way.'

The woman came to the front of the counter. 'Do you know what it is, then? You being a witch an' all?'

The girl sniggered. Alex turned and glared at her. It was all right his thinking Olly silly, but nobody else should laugh at her.

Olly hadn't noticed. 'Oh, no. What you've got here is earth-spirits. Very good for a garden centre. The place should flourish, like the tree in leaf. Keep you all in jobs.'

'Sounds good,' said the woman.

'You should make offerings. Leave cans of

drinks out – and crisps – where they're easy to get at. It'll pay off.'

'I'll be sure to do that,' said the woman, and the girl sniggered again.

As they left the coffee shop, Alex said, 'They didn't believe you. They were laughing at you.'

'Ah, but are there elves in their garden centre, or are there not?'

'There are, but . . .'

'Then who has the last laugh, little pal?' Olly had stopped in front of a display of plastic gnomes. After studying them, she picked one up. It was bending double, turning its head and grinning – leering – over its shoulder. And it was pulling its trousers down and showing a large, rosy bum. Olly carried it to the counter and took out her credit card.

'You're not buying *that*?' Alex said.

'Certain thing, chum.'

'Why?'

'I shall put it in the garden, where it can be seen first thing, on drawing the curtains in the morning.'

'You're daft,' Alex said.

'Not *my* garden, of course.'

'Then whose?'

'Yours.'

'Mine! But the first person up –' Alex began to see it all, and started to grin – 'who opens the curtains – is . . . my mother.'

'Do you think she'll see the joke?'

'No,' Alex said. 'Not at all. Can we get the one that's lifting its kilt as well?'

SUSAN PRICE

# Olly Spellmaker and the Hairy Horror

**Hairy Bill, the helpful bogle, seemed harmless. At first . . .**

Since he arrived at Alex Langford's home, Hairy Bill hasn't stopped polishing and vacuuming. Which means no more chores! But dusting is only the beginning for Hairy Bill – soon he has scary plans to take over the whole house.

When the Langfords call for help, motorbike-riding witch Olly Spellmaker comes to the rescue. With her new bogle-busting assistant, Alex, Olly can handle anything. But she's never had to fight a Hairy Horror!

The first book in the funny, silly, spooky OLLY SPELLMAKER series.

SUSAN PRICE

# Olly Spellmaker and the Sulky Smudge

**The Olde Manor Inne isn't haunted. That's the problem ...**

Olly Spellmaker, the motor-biking witch, has a new assignment: to kit out an unhaunted hotel with ghosts galore! But while Olly knows how to capture spooks, she's not so good at finding them in the first place ...

Olly quickly calls for the help of her reluctant assistant, Alex. With his magical 'twingles' he starts to hunt down some suitable ghouls. Then he discovers a very quiet, grey blob. It seems too feeble to be frightening – but the Sulky Smudge is about to put on a VERY scary show ...

The second book in the funny, silly, spooky OLLY SPELLMAKER series.